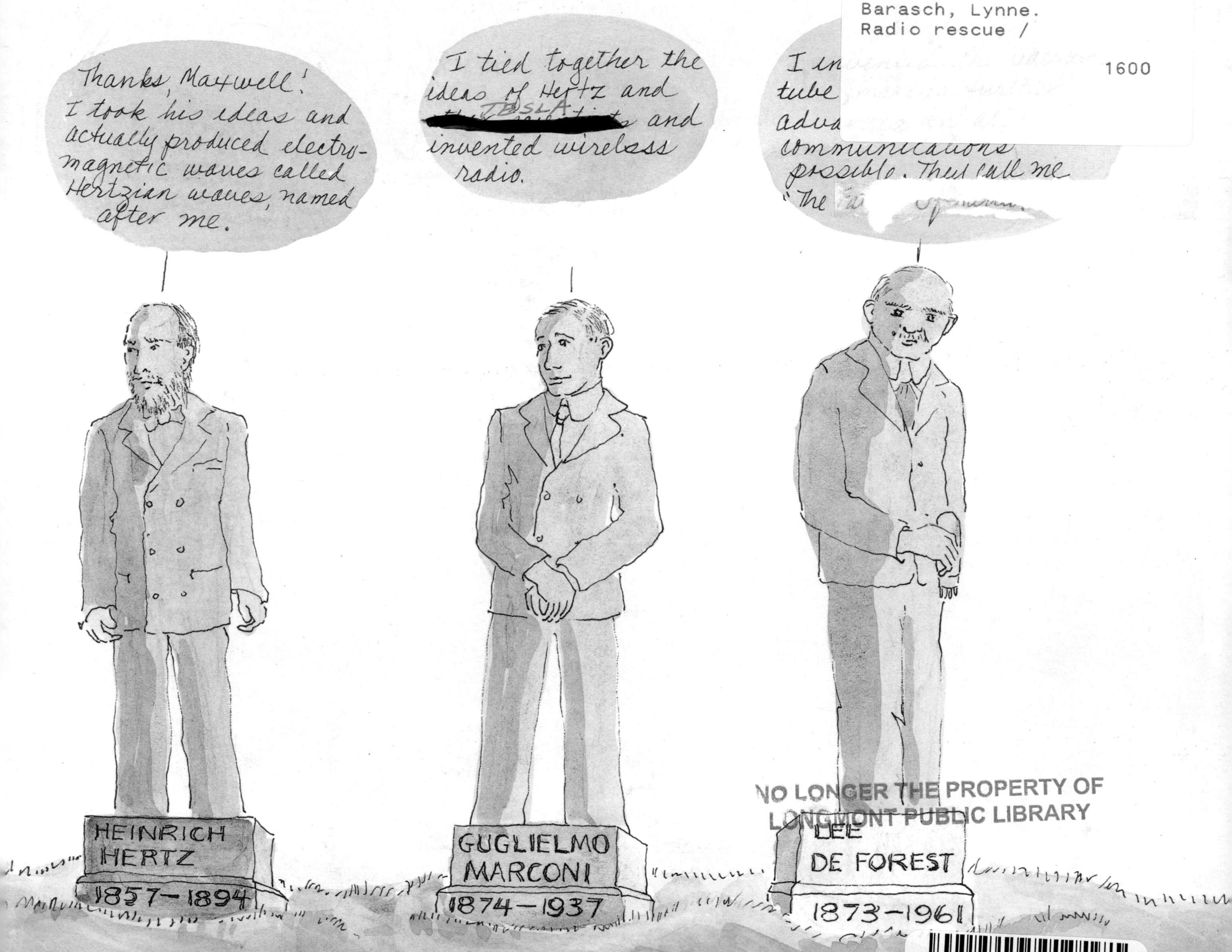

LYNNE BARASCH

RADIO RESCUE

FRANCES FOSTER BOOKS · FARRAR, STRAUS AND GIROUX · NEW YORK

For my parents,
Robert and Elaine Marx

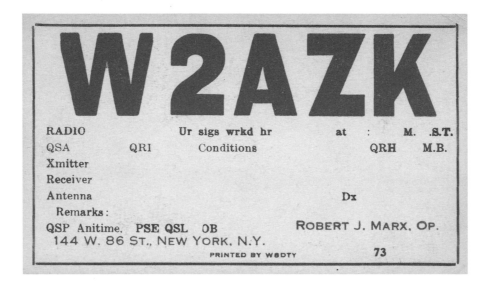

Distributed in Canada by Douglas & McIntyre Ltd.
Color separations by Hong Kong Scanner Arts
Printed and bound in the United States of America by Worzalla
Typography by Judy Lanfredi

First edition, 2000

Library of Congress Cataloging-in-Publication Data

Barasch, Lynne.
    Radio rescue / Lynne Barasch. – 1st ed.
        p.   cm.
    Summary: In the 1920s, after learning Morse code and setting up his own amateur radio station,
a twelve-year-old boy sends a message that leads to the rescue of a family stranded by a hurricane
in Florida. Based on experiences of the author's father.
    ISBN 0-374-36166-5
    [1. Amateur radio stations—Fiction. 2. Morse code—Fiction.]
I. Title.
PZ7.B22965Rad   2000
[Fic]—dc21   99-22384

Author's Note

The boy in this book is actually my father, and the story is based on his experiences as a young amateur radio operator, the youngest to be licensed in the United States at the time. In 1923, when he was ten years old, communicating with someone far away wasn't as easy as it is today. If you wanted to call Los Angeles from New York, you would pick up the phone and say, "Operator, I want to place a person-to-person call to Los Angeles." You would give the operator the name and number you wanted. The operator would then call another operator some miles west of New York. That operator would call the next operator. It might be ten calls before the relay reached Los Angeles. Many hours later, the operator would call you back and say, "Your Los Angeles call is ready." Then you would hear the crackly distant sound of the voice from Los Angeles. If you wanted to call someone in Europe, you were out of luck—overseas phone calls weren't possible at all.

At the same time there was another form of communication that was becoming more and more popular. It was called wireless radio. People all over the world could exchange thoughts and information by sending electronic signals in Morse code through the air using a telegraph key. From the beginning, wireless radio attracted amateur radio operators, who came to be known as hams, and special bands of radio frequencies were designated for their use.

Until recently, Morse code was used on the high seas in ship-to-ship and ship-to-shore radio. All oceangoing cruise ships, by law, were required to have someone on board who was qualified to send and receive Morse code. Airport beacons sent Morse code twenty-four hours a day identifying their locations. So did offshore drilling platforms. During the Vietnam War, in a television interview he was forced to give, American prisoner of war Jeremiah A. Denton, Jr., blinked his eyes to spell out the word TORTURE in Morse code to notify the outside world of his condition. Although Morse code is still used by amateur radio operators and others, international distress calls are now sent by a new satellite system called Global Maritime Distress and Safety System, or GMDSS. Morse code continues to be one of the most reliable forms of communication ever devised.

In 1923, the clothes we wore were prim and proper.

The cars we drove looked like boxes on wheels.

Telephones had no number buttons to press.
You told the operator whom you wanted to call.

And we had a new invention, a way of communicating long-distance through the
air with no wires connecting the callers. It was called wireless radio communication.
You couldn't just talk through the wireless. You had to send messages tapped out in
Morse code with a telegraph key. To do it, you needed a transmitter, a receiver, and
an aerial. Soon aerials were sprouting on rooftops all over the city. I thought it was
wonderful. I was ten years old and itching to get involved.

But first I had to learn Morse code, all the letters of the alphabet and the numbers from 1 to 10. And I'd have to practice tapping the dots and dashes that spelled out the words with a telegraph key. A dot, or short sound, was made by pushing down and releasing the telegraph key quickly. For a dash, you held the key down longer, making a long sound. Each different combination of dots and dashes makes a different letter or number.

I lived in a small apartment on the Upper West Side of New York City with my mother and our dog, Fly. There wasn't much room, so when I bought my secondhand receiver and earphones, I put them right in my bedroom. I would not be allowed to send Morse code until I got my amateur, or ham, license and a radio transmitter. But with my receiver and earphones I could dial up and down the frequencies and listen to other people sending Morse code. A single wire ran from my window to the roof, the only aerial this simple setup needed.

I studied code a few letters at a time. I began to tap out words with my fingers on any surface I could find—while walking down the street, riding on the bus, going to and from school, everywhere I went.

At home, I listened to traffic on the air. Slowly I was learning to decode. One day I picked up 2CUQ with my receiver. I knew that these were a licensed operator's call letters, or ID, so I looked them up in my amateur radio, or ham, directory. They belonged to Bill Irwin, who lived only seven blocks away from me. I called him on the telephone and we made plans to meet. Bill was seventeen and already had his ham radio license, which he called his "ticket."

Late one night, Bill noticed smoke coming in his window. Flames were shooting from the third floor of the building next door. He grabbed the phone, but the line was dead.

Going quickly to his telegraph key, he raised another ham operator and tapped out FIRE AT 114 W 74 CALL FIRE DEPT RUSH. The message got through.

A few minutes later, a fire truck came.

The firemen hoisted a ladder and carried a mother and baby down to safety.

How I wanted my chance to go on the air! But I was barely able to read code.

Would I ever be good enough to take the test for a license?

Bill gave me his old notebook to help me study, but he warned, "Don't expect a rescue every day. It hardly ever happens."

As if it weren't hard enough to learn Morse code, here in Bill's notebook was another code within the code, abbreviations for faster transmission and international signals that all began with the letter Q and could be understood in any language. How would I ever sort it all out? "Dot by dot and dash by dash," Bill joked. Then he laughed and said, "Didididit didit." It wasn't until I read the notebook that I discovered what that meant. Laughter in Morse code!

Finally, I went down to the Custom House to take the test. I only had to read ten words per minute, not send any code. But I failed it. Leaving the building, I cried all the way down the steps. Even though I could take the test again anytime, I knew it would be a long while before I would be ready.

For the next year I studied and practiced until even my dreams were in Morse code. I could recognize whole words and phrases at a time. The code had become a language I could understand at last.

When I took the test again, I passed.

I was now a licensed operator. I had my ticket,
just like Bill, and my very own call letters.
They were 2AZK.

Bill had promised to help me set up my station when I got my license. All of us hams built our stations ourselves from scratch. We called them our shacks. Bill said, "Wait till you see Cortlandt Street!" We took the subway downtown.

Store after store was jam-packed with radio equipment that spilled out onto tables in front. There were vacuum tubes used to amplify sound; bus bar wire for building circuits; lengths of rubber covering, called spaghetti, to prevent one wire from touching another; soldering irons; motor generators to boost power for better transmission; batteries that yielded direct current for pure power; braided wire for aerials; telegraph keys; and earphones.

We returned home with armloads of stuff,
unwrapped the packages, and went right to work.

We built a circuit, soldering it together so it could activate the UV 845 vacuum tube for
my transmitter. Then we mounted it on the back of the large master panel, with the
meters showing through, and stood it in the corner by the window.

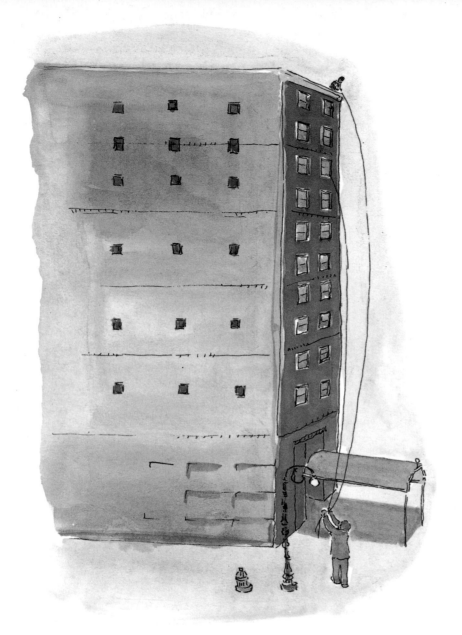

The aerial was next. I knew it would have to be strung over the street away from the wall of my building where the steel would interfere with the radio reception. Frank Betz, the super from the building across the street, was my friend. He knew all about my radio efforts and said he'd help. Together we made a plan. One night, when the traffic had quieted down, I went up to the roof. I attached a wire firmly to a railing and dropped the other end down to Frank, who was waiting below on the street. I had also hung a wire from my eighth-story bedroom window, which Frank attached to the dropped wire. Frank tied the wires to a rope that was fastened to the railing of his roof and hoisted it high over the street to his rooftop.

My first call was a local one. Guess who!

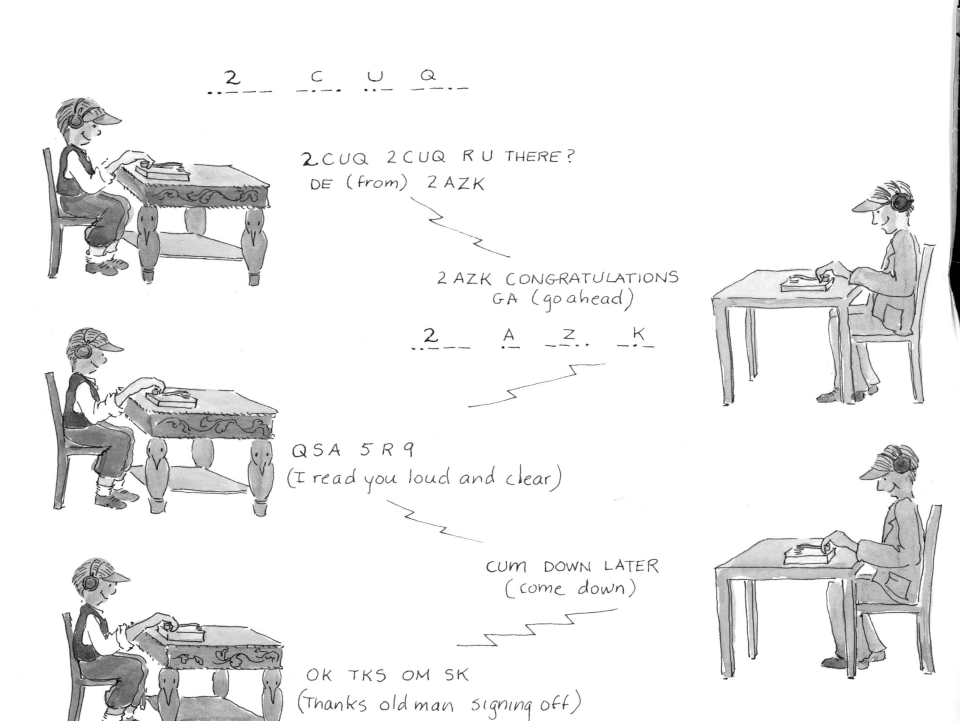

It formed a slanted T-shaped aerial. My station was complete.
Now 2AZK could be on the air!

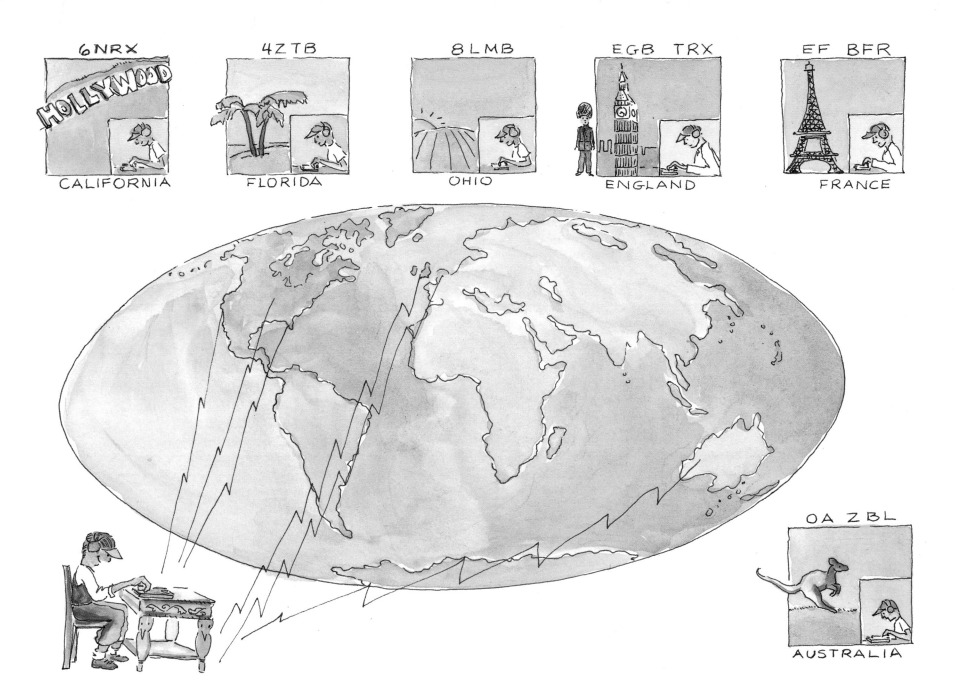

In the months that followed, I went on to call California, Florida, Ohio, and then England, France, and even Australia. I sent CQ, the general call, then DX, meaning that I was looking for someone from a distance, and then my call letters, 2AZK, and then I'd wait to hear a response. If I heard my call letters repeated, I'd know I'd raised someone. I looked forward to hearing world news every day. The foreign stations and I would plan to meet again on the air at a regular prearranged time.

One night I noticed flashes of light coming from the navy ships anchored in the Hudson River. They were sending code back and forth from one ship to the other, beginning with a series of dits.

I got out my flashlight and went up to the roof, where, instead of sending CQ, the usual way to open a communication, I sent the same series of dits and then my call letters, 2AZK.

Soon I was exchanging messages in code with dozens of sailors. They asked if I would make phone calls for them, to tell their families and girlfriends when they'd be home on shore leave.

Once ashore, the sailors paid me a visit. They weren't expecting a twelve-year-old boy! My mother was surprised, too. She hadn't known about my rooftop signaling.

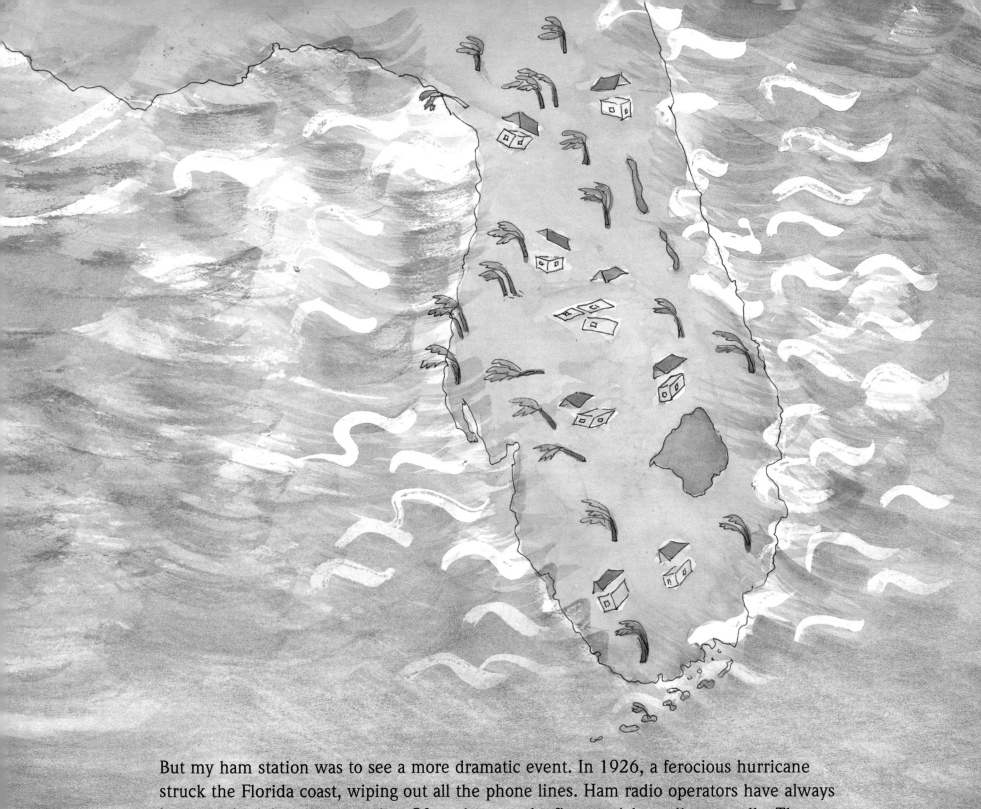

But my ham station was to see a more dramatic event. In 1926, a ferocious hurricane struck the Florida coast, wiping out all the phone lines. Ham radio operators have always been on the job in emergencies. Often they are the first to pick up distress calls. The Coast Guard radio was completely tied up handling local rescue operations, leaving ham radio as the only way for outsiders to get news from the disaster area.

I sat glued to my receiver, listening to traffic, when I picked up a message from 4LDG in Miami. 4LDG was transmitting the names of people who had survived the storm and wanted to tell family and friends in New York that they were safe.

I carefully wrote down all the names to call, thinking that was the end of the message. But it wasn't. Just as I was ready to sign off, I heard FAMILY STRANDED IN FLOOD ON KEY LARGO·QSB (SIGNAL FADING) PLES CALL COAST GUARD, and he signed off.

I tried to raise the Coast Guard on ordinary channels but couldn't get through. I kept thinking about the family on Key Largo. Maybe they had a boy like me, maybe a dog like mine. Maybe they were huddled on the roof of a house waiting for a rescue. It was against the law, but I got on the emergency band reserved for official use and sent: SOS FAMILY STRANDED ON KEY LARGO EXACT LOCATION UNKNOWN SEND HELP RUSH. I sent that message over and over.

Finally the Coast Guard in Miami acknowledged. It would send a boat out to look for the family.

I stayed on the air most of the night relaying more hurricane news until finally the Coast Guard in Miami broke in with FAMILY ON KEY LARGO SAFE TKS TO U. In spite of my excitement, I signed off and went to sleep. I had been working traffic for twenty-four hours!

A few days later, a reporter came to interview me and take a picture of me and my shack.

INFANT RADIO OPERATOR TALKS TO TWELVE FOREIGN STATIONS NIGHTLY

I wasn't too happy about being called an infant, and there was no mention of the hurricane rescue, but I didn't mind. We ham radio operators like nothing better than to help whenever there is a disaster. I was proud to be a small part of that great tradition.

INTERNATIONAL MORSE CODE

A	·—	N	—·	1	·————
B	—···	O	———	2	··———
C	—·—·	P	·——·	3	···——
D	—··	Q	——·—		
E	·	R	·—·	4	····—
F	··—·	S	···	5	·····
G	——·	T	—	6	—····
H	····	U	··—		
I	··	V	···—	7	——···
J	·———	W	·——	8	———··
K	—·—	X	—··—	9	————·
L	·—··	Y	—·——	0	—————
M	——	Z	——··